This book belongs to

_____

Bluebell Glade

Dandelion Dell

Heart of Misty Wo

Hawthorn Hedgerows

Heather Hill

Sundown Hill

Crystal Cave

Golden Meadow

Moonshine Pond

Dewdrop Spring

Honeydew Meadow

Mulberry Bushes

Misty Wood Rabbit Warren

HOME
SWEET
HOME

How many *Fairy Animals* books
have you collected?

 Chloe the Kitten

 Bella the Bunny

 Paddy the Puppy

 Mia the Mouse

And there are lots more magical
adventures coming very soon!

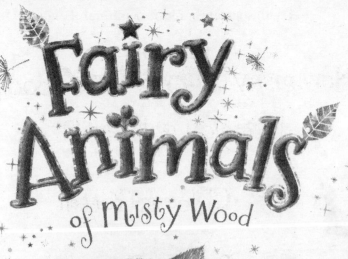

Fairy Animals
of Misty Wood

Chloe the Kitten

Lily Small

EGMONT

With special thanks to Susannah Leigh.

EGMONT
We bring stories to life

Chloe the Kitten first published in Great Britain 2013
by Egmont UK Limited
The Yellow Building, 1 Nicholas Road, London W11 4AN

Text copyright © 2013 Hothouse Fiction Ltd
Illustrations copyright © 2013 Kirsteen Harris Jones
All rights reserved

The moral rights of the illustrator have been asserted

ISBN 978 1 4052 6034 3
1 3 5 7 9 10 8 6 4 2

www.egmont.co.uk

www.hothousefiction.com

www.fairyanimals.com

A CIP catalogue record for this title is available from the British Library

Printed and bound in Great Britain by The CPI Group

50044/1

FSC — MIX Paper — FSC® C018306

EGMONT LUCKY COIN

Our story began over a century ago, when seventeen-year-old Egmont Harald Petersen found a coin in the street.

He was on his way to buy a flyswatter, a small hand-operated printing machine that he then set up in his tiny apartment.

The coin brought him such good luck that today Egmont has offices in over 30 countries around the world. And that lucky coin is still kept at the company's head offices in Denmark.

Contents

CHAPTER ONE

Good Morning, Misty Wood

It was early morning in Misty Wood.
The moon had long since snuggled
into his starry bed, and the sun
was just beginning to stretch into

the sky. In a cosy cot made from moss and grass, in a tiny home, tucked under the roots of an old chestnut tree, a kitten called Chloe was waking up.

She yawned and rubbed the
end of her nose with a velvety paw.
Then she opened her eyes and
looked at her dandelion clock.

'Oh, no! I'm late!' she cried,
leaping from her bed. But she
stopped short when she caught
sight of herself in the small pool
of water she used as a mirror.
'Puppy tails and poppy seeds!'
she meowed. 'I can't go out
like this!'

Chloe's whiskers were flat from where she had slept on them. Quickly, she licked her paws and stroked her whiskers until they were shiny and smooth. Then she twisted her head and looked down to check her glittery fairy wings.

You see, Chloe was no ordinary kitten. She was a Cobweb Kitten, one of the many fairy animals who lived in Misty Wood.

Every fairy animal in Misty

Wood had a special job to do
to make sure it stayed such a
wonderful place. The Bud Bunnies
used their twitchy noses to ease
flowers into bloom. The Hedgerow
Hedgehogs used their spikes
to pick up leaves and keep the
ground tidy The Holly Hamsters
nibbled the holly leaves into
shape for Christmas. It was the
Cobweb Kittens' job to decorate
the cobwebs in the wood with

glistening dewdrops so that they sparkled and shone.

Chloe patted her wings into place and smiled.

'Perfect,' she purred. 'Now I'm ready for work.'

She picked up her special dewdrop-collecting basket, which had been woven from flower stems. 'No time for breakfast today,' she said, looking over longingly at the acorn cup of milk on her

conker table. The magical spring where the Cobweb Kittens got their dewdrops only came to life while the sun was rising. She had to get there quickly or she would miss it.

Chloe padded across to the door and pushed it open. Outside, it was as if Misty Wood was just stirring itself from sleep. A breeze whispered through the trees, making all the branches sway.

Chloe could hear the first chirps of the birds as they got ready to sing. She opened her wings and they shimmered purple and pink in the first morning light.

'Good morning, Misty Wood!' she said, fluttering up into the air.

Chloe swooped through the trees and out into Bluebell Glade. Down below her she could hear the tinkle of hundreds of flowery bells as they bobbed in the breeze.

GOOD MORNING, MISTY WOOD

She breathed in the bluebells'
sweet scent and carried on her way.

As she left the glade she came
to Heather Hill. *It matches my wings*,
Chloe thought to herself with a
smile as she looked down at the
purple carpet of heather.

Next she did a loop-the-loop
over Golden Meadow, hoping to
catch sight of the playful Pollen
Puppies flicking the golden flower
pollen with their tails. But the

cheeky pups were asleep, curled up on their cushions of moss.

Chloe floated on, enjoying the sleepy silence. The meadow below her looked like a rainbow that had been painted across the land. There were flowers of every colour.

Then she came to Moonshine Pond. The Moonbeam Moles had been working hard all night, flying through the sky and dropping moonbeams into the pond to

make it look pretty. Now the water had a beautiful pearly glow. It reminded Chloe of the cup of milk in her kitchen and she suddenly felt very thirsty. She looked at the brightening sky. The sun wasn't quite up yet. As long as she was quick she should have enough time for a drink.

Chloe flew down and landed on the soft bank of the pond. Putting her basket next to her, she

leaned forwards to lap the sweet
water with her tiny pink tongue.
She was careful to be as quiet as
can be.

She didn't want to wake the little moles, as they would only just have gone to bed.

Mmm, Chloe thought, *that's better!* The water was delicious. The moonbeams made it taste as sweet as honey. Chloe licked her lips, unfurled her wings and fluttered off again.

At last she came to a beautiful valley. In the middle of the valley lay a shimmering lake. Silvery mist

drifted across the surface of
the water. Suddenly, as the first
rays of sunlight peeped over the
treetops and touched the lake, a jet
of water rose high into the air, like
a fountain. Fat, glistening
dewdrops fell down like sparkles
from a fairy's wand. Chloe
breathed a sigh of relief. She had
arrived at Dewdrop Spring just
in time.

The air was filled with excited

meowing and purring. There were Cobweb Kittens everywhere! Fluttering their wings as fast as they could, they headed towards the spring, scooping up dewdrops in their special collecting baskets. Every kitten needed to work very hard if all the cobwebs in Misty Wood were to be covered in dewdrops.

'Hello, Chloe,' a little tabby kitten called as he flew past.

16

'Hurry up, you're late!' a white kitten cried, her fairy wings glistening silver and gold.

'Here I come!' Chloe called happily to her friends. 'Save some for me!' With a flick of her wings she dived towards the fountain ready to collect the dewdrops with her basket.

But as she held out her paws, she noticed something terrible.

Her basket was missing!

CHAPTER TWO
A Helpful Friend

Chloe gave a sad little meow.

What could have happened to her

basket? Then she remembered.

She had set it down on the bank of

Moonshine Pond when she stopped

for a drink. She must have forgotten to pick it up again.

'Whiskers and whirlpools! Whatever am I going to do?' Chloe cried. She looked anxiously at the sky. It was getting lighter and lighter! There was no time for her to go all the way back to Moonshine Pond. Soon the sun would be up and Dewdrop Spring would disappear

for another day. Then there would

be no dewdrops for her to collect

and she wouldn't be able to

decorate her cobwebs.

She watched as, one by one,

the other Cobweb Kittens filled

their baskets and flew away. Her

cobwebs would be the only empty

ones in all of Misty Wood!

Chloe flopped down on to a

patch of grass and put her fluffy

head in her paws. A tear trickled

slowly down her nose.

'If I can't decorate my cobwebs I'll be the worst Cobweb Kitten ever,' she sobbed.

'And why can't you decorate your cobwebs?' a cheery voice asked from behind her.

Chloe turned and peeked out from between her paws. A Stardust Squirrel was sitting on a log in front of her, holding an acorn. Chloe sighed. Normally she

would be pleased to see a Stardust Squirrel. They were some of the most beautiful creatures in Misty Wood. Their soft fur was a glittery grey or dusky red colour and their wings were very delicate. When they shook their bushy tails, they sent a shimmer of stardust floating over all the leaves in the wood, making them glimmer and sparkle.

'I left my basket at Moonshine Pond,' Chloe whispered. 'Now I

can't collect any dewdrops.'

'And why did you leave your basket at Moonshine Pond?' the squirrel asked with a twirl of his whiskers.

'Because I'd put it down so I could have a drink,' Chloe said, feeling very ashamed.

'I see,' said the squirrel. 'And why did you need a drink?'

'Because I didn't have any breakfast.'

'Oh, you must never leave the house without having breakfast,' the squirrel said with a twinkle in his eye. He hopped off the log and bounded over to Chloe, leaving a glittery trail behind him. 'I always have a bowl of acorns for breakfast. I was just collecting some actually.' The squirrel held out his acorn to her. 'Here, do you want one?'

Chloe shook her head.

The squirrel looked thoughtful for a moment. 'What you really need is a walnut,' he said.

'No, thank you. I'm much too sad to be hungry,' Chloe replied.

The Stardust Squirrel gave a gentle laugh. It sounded like the tinkle of ice crystals on a frozen lake. 'I don't mean to eat,' he said. 'I mean to make a basket.'

Chloe frowned. How could she use a walnut as a basket?

CHLOE THE KITTEN

'Wait here,' the squirrel said. Chloe watched as he scampered over to a small tree stump on the banks of the lake, scattering a trail of stardust as he ran.

'Ta da!' he cried, rummaging around in the tree stump. 'Just the thing!' He pulled out half a walnut shell.

Chloe looked at the wrinkled shell. 'That doesn't look much like a basket,' she said sadly.

'Not yet,' the squirrel agreed. 'But just you watch.'

Quick as a flash, the squirrel nibbled two little holes in the side of the shell. Then he picked a thick blade of grass and, with a blur of paws and a flurry of stardust, he tied the grass to the walnut shell to make a perfect handle.

'Oh, I see!' Chloe exclaimed. 'It's a perfect dewdrop-collecting basket. Thank you!'

'You're welcome,' said the squirrel. 'Now, are you sure you don't want this tasty acorn?'

Chloe smiled and shook her head. 'No, thank you, I've got

work to do. Goodbye!' And with that she flew up into the air and over to the spring.

Flapping her wings hard, Chloe swooped this way and that, catching glistening dewdrops as she flew. The walnut shell was bigger than her old basket, so she was able to collect more drops than ever before. Just as Chloe had filled her basket, the sun finished rising above the trees. At once,

Dewdrop Spring sank back into the lake.

'Just in time,' Chloe said to herself as she fluttered through the valley and off to Hawthorn Hedgerows, the part of Misty Wood she was in charge of decorating.

Hawthorn Hedgerows were right by the edge of the wood. As Chloe flew closer, she spotted the silvery strings of a

33

delicate cobweb clinging to the first hedge. She shivered with excitement. She would soon make it look beautiful.

'I have just the dewdrops for you,' Chloe said with a smile as she hovered close to the web. She chose the smallest and sparkliest dewdrops from her basket and carefully hung them one by one on the threads.

When she had filled the

cobweb with dewdrops she flew back a bit to check her work. The cobweb now sparkled like a jewel! Eagerly, Chloe flew over to the next web and began again. As she worked, she hummed a little tune. She felt so glad to be able to decorate her cobwebs after all.

Chloe was starting her fifth cobweb when she felt a gentle tap on the top of her head. She looked up to see a small spider dangling

above her on a strand of silky web.

'Sorry to trouble you,' the

spider said, pointing a spindly

leg towards the part of the hedge Chloe had just finished. 'But I was wondering why you haven't decorated my web?'

'I have!' Chloe answered in surprise. 'Look, I'll show you.'

She spread her wings and flew back along the hedge. But to her dismay she saw that the spider was right. His cobweb was empty! There were no dewdrops on it at all. And all of the other

37

cobwebs Chloe had spent so long

decorating were bare too.

Her dewdrops had completely

disappeared!

CHAPTER THREE

The Dewdrop Thief

Chloe flew this way and that, searching for the dewdrops. They were nowhere to be seen.

'I told you,' the spider said, solemnly blinking his tiny eyes.

'But I just don't understand!' Chloe meowed. 'I'm sure I did that cobweb. Look, it was the same as this one.'

Chloe turned to show the spider the web she had just begun to decorate with sparkly dewdrops. But, to her surprise, they had gone too!

'Someone must have stolen them!' Chloe cried. She gulped. Someone . . . or some*thing*.

'You mean we have a dewdrop thief?' the spider asked, frowning.

Chloe nodded. 'I'm afraid so.'

'I don't like the sound of that,' said the spider, and he scuttled off as fast as his eight legs would carry him.

Chloe slumped down on to the ground. 'Whatever will I tell all the other fairy animals?' she sighed. 'They will think I haven't done any work at all this morning.'

She gazed gloomily into her

basket. There were lots of lovely plump dewdrops left, but if she hung them up, would they just disappear too?

Then Chloe had a brilliant idea. 'Cockleshells and conkers!' she cried with a grin. 'I know what I'll do.'

Carefully, she lifted out a shimmering dewdrop from her basket. She placed it gently on a silky strand of the nearest cobweb.

Then she added two more dewdrops so that all three hung in
a row, sparkling like precious
jewels.

'Ah, well,' Chloe declared
loudly. 'I think it's time I went and
had some breakfast.' She gave her
tummy a pat. 'Ooh, I'm so hungry.'

44

Chloe unfurled her wings and started to fly away. But instead of leaving Hawthorn Hedgerows, she swerved round the back of a large oak tree. Chloe was well hidden behind its huge trunk, but if she peeked out she had a perfect view of the cobweb she had just decorated.

'Now all I have to do is wait,' she said to herself, 'and see if the dewdrop thief comes back.'

Chloe waited. And as she waited she began to wonder if her idea had been such a good one after all.

What if the dewdrop thief is very big? she thought.

The branches of the old oak tree creaked.

What if the dewdrop thief is very scary?

A breeze shivered through the leaves.

What if the dewdrop thief doesn't like Cobweb Kittens?

There was a rustling in the hedgerow. Chloe peered further round the tree. The thread of the silvery web was trembling and the

47

dewdrops were quivering.

Was the thief coming?

Chloe crouched back down in her hiding place, not daring to look.

The rustling stopped and there was silence. Gathering up all of her courage, Chloe peeped out.

What she saw wasn't big.

And it wasn't scary.

There, in the middle of the clearing, was a tiny Moss Mouse.

Moss Mice were another type of
fairy animal. Their special job
was to shape Misty Wood's moss
into velvety cushions for the other
animals to sleep on. But this timid
creature looked much too small for
any kind of job. He was just
a baby!

For a moment the mouse
sat all alone in the middle of the
clearing. Then he tiptoed over to
the hedge. With a flutter of his tiny
wings he flew up to the cobweb
and began lapping thirstily at the
nearest dewdrop.

Chloe stared in disbelief. To
think that she had been scared of a
terrible thief when all the time her
hard work was being slurped up
by a greedy mouse!

'What are you doing?' she cried, flying out from her hiding place.

The little Moss Mouse was so startled he fell backwards from the web, did a somersault and landed with a plop on a toadstool below. The dewdrops splashed down on top of him like rain.

'Those dewdrops aren't for drinking. They're to make the hedges look pretty,' Chloe went on.

'I spent ages hanging them.'

But as she hovered above the Moss Mouse she saw that the water running down his pointy nose wasn't from the dewdrops. Big, splashy tears were spilling from his eyes and soaking his downy cheeks.

'I'm sorry,' the little mouse said in a trembly voice. 'But I was very thirsty and I didn't know where else to get a drink.'

He put his head in his tiny
paws and sobbed some more.

Chloe felt awful. He was such
a young mouse, and he looked so
sad. She shouldn't have got cross
with him.

'It's all right,' Chloe purred,
patting his back with her paw. 'I'm
sorry I shouted at you. What's
your name, and why are you so
thirsty?'

'My name is Morris,' the

mouse sniffed. 'I'm thirsty because I – I –' he started to cry again. 'I lost my mummy and daddy.'

'You *lost* them?' Chloe asked.

Morris nodded sadly.

'How did you lose them?'

Morris looked down at the floor. 'We were going to visit Grandma,' he whispered, 'and I flew off to look at some buttercups. And then . . . and then . . . well, I couldn't find my way back.' He let

out another sob.

Chloe picked a velvety leaf from the hedge next to them and handed it to him. 'Here,' she said. 'Wipe your eyes.'

Morris dabbed at his face with the leaf.

'When did you lose your mummy and daddy?' Chloe asked.

'Yesterday morning,' Morris replied.

CHLOE THE KITTEN

'Yesterday morning?' Chloe stared at him. 'No wonder you're thirsty.'

'I was only going to drink one dewdrop,' Morris whimpered, 'but they were so tasty. I'm sorry.' He hung his head again.

Chloe thought of how the Stardust Squirrel had helped her when she'd lost her basket. Now it was her turn to help.

'Don't worry,' she said with

57

a smile. 'I'll help you find your mummy and daddy, I promise. Do you have any idea where your home is?'

Morris nodded. 'It's by the lions.'

Chloe stared at him in shock. 'By the *lions*?'

'Yes,' the little mouse replied. 'By the big lions.'

Chloe gave a gulp of dismay. She didn't know there were lions

in Misty Wood. Her heart began to pound. Finding Morris's home might be a lot scarier than she had thought!

CHAPTER FOUR
The Rainbow Slide

Morris looked up at Chloe. His shiny black eyes blinked at her anxiously. 'Please will you take me home?' he squeaked. 'I miss my mummy and daddy.'

Chloe's tummy gave a little lurch. She had to keep her promise. It was up to her to get Morris back safely, however scary it might be.

'Ladybirds and lollipops!' she whispered to herself. 'If this little mouse is brave enough to live next door to some big lions then, as sure as my wings are purple, I am brave enough to take him there.'

She turned to Morris again. 'Is your home very far away?'

'Oh, yes. Miles and miles,' Morris replied.

'In that case,' Chloe said, 'I think it would be better if I carried you. Your wings are so small and you must be very tired. Why don't you climb on to my back? We'll fly above Misty Wood together. You can help me look out for the lions.'

Morris clapped his tiny paws. 'Thank you! Thank you!' he squeaked excitedly.

Chloe tucked her basket of dewdrops beneath a hedge to keep it safe. Then she crouched down low and Morris clambered on to her back and perched between her wings. 'Now, hold on tight!' Chloe called.

With a flick of her shimmering wings she flew up into the sky, brushing the treetops with her sparkly tail as she rose higher and higher.

'Wheeeeeeeee!' Morris cried.

Far below, Misty Wood lay stretched out like a colourful patchwork quilt, glimmering in the early morning sunshine. Somewhere down there, in amongst the meadows and the mountains, the grasslands and the glades, Morris's family were waiting anxiously for him.

But where were they?

A scamper of golden fur across

a patch of brilliant blue caught Chloe's eye.

Lions?

Chloe caught her breath and peered closer.

No, it was only the Pollen Puppies. They were awake and playing in Bluebell Glade, flicking the pollen here and there with their tails so that even more flowers would grow.

I wonder if they know where the

lions live? Chloe thought to herself. She called over her shoulder to her tiny passenger. 'Hold on, Morris! We're going down!'

With a flutter of fairy wings, Chloe landed in the glade.

'Hey! What's going on?' Petey, a floppy-eared puppy cried as he bounced over.

'Have you come to play with us?' his friend Paddy asked as he

scampered up. Clouds of yellow pollen fell like gold dust from his coat. 'Look, everyone – it's a Cobweb Kitten who wants to be a Pollen Puppy!'

'No, I don't wa–' Chloe began, but Paddy was already running round her, his tail wagging.

'First of all you have to learn how to bark,' Paddy said. 'Show her how to bark, Petey.'

69

'But I don't –' Chloe spluttered, but before she could say any more, Petey started barking.

'And wag your tail,' Paddy called. 'You have to wag your tail if you want to be a Pollen Puppy. It's what we do best.'

Petey barked even louder and other puppies started joining in too, until the whole glade became a blur of wagging tails and barking puppies.

'But –' said Chloe.

'Oh, dear,' squeaked Morris.

'I DON'T WANT TO BARK AND I DON'T WANT TO WAG MY TAIL AND I DON'T WANT TO BE A POLLEN PUPPY!' Chloe shouted at the top of her voice. The glade fell silent.

'Oh,' said Petey.

'No need to shout,' sniffed Paddy.

'I'm sorry,' said Chloe. 'I'm

72

sure it's great fun being a Pollen Puppy, but something very sad has happened and I need your help.'

'Well, why didn't you say so?' said Paddy.

'What's happened?' asked Petey.

'When I was hanging up my dewdrops this morning I found this little mouse.' Chloe gestured with her paw. The puppies, who hadn't noticed Morris because he was so small, gathered closer. 'His

73

name is Morris and he got lost
on the way to his grandma's, so
I'm helping him find his way back
home. But . . .' Chloe gulped and
dropped her voice to a whisper . . .
'Morris says he lives near some
lions! Do you know if there are
any lions living in Misty Wood?'

'Lions?' A spotty puppy
called Pepper started to laugh.
'Has anyone seen any lions?'

'Grrr!' Paddy bared his tiny

74

white teeth.

'Growl!' Petey sharpened his
pointy claws.

'Roar!' Pepper shook her head
so the pollen floated around her
ears like a golden mane.

'Lions you say? Here we are!'

Chloe shook her head crossly. Usually the cheeky Pollen Puppies made her laugh, but this was no time for joking. She had to get Morris home.

'Please can you help me?' she begged. 'Morris has been lost for a very long time.'

At the sound of Chloe's sad voice the puppies stopped their teasing.

'Sorry,' said Paddy. 'We were only joking.'

'We really don't know where the lions live,' Petey piped up.

'Hmm,' said Pepper. 'Why don't you try looking in Crystal Cave at the side of Heather Hill?'

'Crystal Cave? That's a great idea!' Chloe cried.

'You know how to get there, don't you?' said Paddy. 'Just follow the rainbow.'

'Thank you, puppies,' Chloe said with a smile. 'Hold on tight, Morris. We're going up again!'

'Good bye! Good luck!' the Pollen Puppies called, their furry tails waving wildly.

'And if you do ever want to be a Pollen Puppy, just let us know,' Paddy called out.

Crystal Cave was tucked away on the very darkest side of Heather

Hill. Chloe knew exactly where to go. Usually the sight of her favourite hill, covered with pretty purple flowers, made her feel so happy. Today, however, she felt scared. She had never seen a lion before, but she knew they were the biggest members of the cat family. *And a Cobweb Kitten is the smallest*, she thought nervously. Now someone even smaller needed her help. Morris was counting on

her to find his mummy and daddy.
She couldn't let him down.

Suddenly there was a tiny
shout in her left ear.

'Look, Chloe!' Morris cried.
'A rainbow! A rainbow!'

Sure enough, a rainbow of
sparkling light arched across the
sky in front of them. Chloe flapped
her glittery wings with all her
might until she landed on the very
top of the rainbow. 'Hold tight,

Morris, we're going for a ride!' she called over her shoulder.

'Wheeeeeeeee!' Morris cried as they started to slide down the rainbow.

Faster and faster they slid. Chloe's whiskers tingled as the air whistled through them. Finally, they landed with a soft bump on the far side of Heather Hill, right at the mouth of Crystal Cave.

The warm colours of the

CHLOE THE KITTEN

crystals in the cave shimmered
across Chloe's fur like fairy lights.
For a moment she almost forgot
what she was looking for. The
rainbow ride had been so much
fun and Crystal Cave was so
pretty, it couldn't possibly be home
to anything scary. Could it?

Suddenly a very deep voice
boomed out from the depths of
the cave. 'Who's there?'

Chloe fell back in fright.

'What do you want?' the voice rang out again.

Chloe crouched down. She was terrified. On her back, Morris gave a small squeal and cowered into her trembling fur.

A dark shadow loomed out of the cave. Chloe could hardly bear to look.

Were the Pollen Puppies right?

Could this be the hiding place of a large and scary lion?

CHAPTER FIVE
The Crystal Cave

'Well?' the voice boomed again.

'I said, who's there?'

Chloe blinked against the dazzling light.

'Oh!' she cried. 'You're . . .'

'I'm what?' the figure boomed.

'You're not a lion!'

'Of course I'm not a lion!'

Chloe laughed with relief as the figure emerged. Now he was standing in the sunlight she could see he wasn't anything like a lion. He was a Bark Badger. From his broad black-and-white shoulders sprouted a pair of delicate, greying wings. The stocky creature

shuffled forwards and frowned down at them.

'Well,' he said. 'What do you little 'uns want? Apart from to tell me that I'm not a lion!'

Chloe opened her mouth, but no sound came out. She may not have been face-to-face with a lion, but she *was* still a bit scared. Bark Badgers were very kind fairy animals, but they were also very big and strong. Their nimble paws

carved the most beautiful patterns into the tree barks of Misty Wood and they took their job very seriously indeed. Unlike the cheeky Pollen Puppies, they had no time for jokes or tricks.

Gathering all of her courage, Chloe raised her head and began to speak.

'I'm helping this little Moss Mouse,' she said with a trembling voice. 'He's lost and I'm trying to

88

find his home. He says it's near the lions but I have no idea where the lions live. The Pollen Puppies suggested I try looking here.'

'Hmmmm.' The Bark Badger stroked his whiskery chin thoughtfully. 'Lions, you say?'

Chloe nodded.

'I have lived in Misty Wood forever and a day, and I have never known there to be lions here,' the Bark Badger said.

'Oh, bother and broomsticks,' Chloe said with a sad sigh. 'Will I ever get Morris home?'

The Bark Badger's wise black eyes began to twinkle. 'I can see you are a very helpful and caring kitten,' he said. 'So I will give you

some advice. Are you listening carefully?'

Chloe leaned forwards.

'Oh, yes,' she said eagerly.

'There is a place in Misty Wood that is very dark and very quiet,' the Bark Badger whispered in her ear. 'No birds sing. No squirrels scamper. Everything is silent and still. It is in the Heart of Misty Wood, and few have ever been there.' He tapped the side

of his nose knowingly with a long pointy claw. 'If there are lions in Misty Wood, that is where they will be hiding.'

Chloe gave a small meow of fear. 'Really, truly?' she whispered.

'Really, truly.' The Bark Badger nodded.

'Oh. Well. Thank you,' Chloe squeaked, trying to look braver than she felt. Her mind was racing.

She had never ventured into
the Heart of Misty Wood before.
It sounded very dark. And very
scary.

'What did he say? What did
he say?' Morris squeaked from her
back.

'He said we are close to
finding your home,' Chloe replied.
She couldn't let Morris know how
nervous she was.

'Yippee! Yippee!' Morris cried

and did a little somersault somewhere behind Chloe's ear.

'Well, we'd better be off then.' Chloe smiled bravely at the Bark Badger. 'Here I go. Into the Heart of Misty Wood.'

She paused.

'Into the darkness,' she went on, her voice wobbling ever so slightly.

'Perhaps you would like something to light your way?'

the Bark Badger suggested.

Chloe smiled. 'Oh, yes please.'

The Bark Badger shuffled back into his cave and soon returned with a piece of crystal taken from the roof of the cave. It glowed with so many different colours it was as if he was holding a piece of rainbow.

'Thank you. It's so beautiful,' Chloe breathed.

'You're welcome,' the badger
replied. 'Now, hold it carefully
ahead of you and let the light
show you the way. Goodbye.'
The Bark Badger waved a large

paw at them. 'And good luck!'

Chloe flew up into the air, clutching the crystal light tightly in her front paws.

'Goodbye, Mr Bark Badger!' she called. 'And thank you again!'

Soon they had left the beauty of the Crystal Cave far behind and were venturing deeper into Misty Wood. Chloe held the rainbow crystal before her. Its warm glow lit up the

97

gloom, but also cast shadows that darted amongst the tree trunks. Sometimes it looked as if strange shapes were following them as they flew.

'It's so dark,' Morris squeaked. 'And scary too.'

'It's only the light playing tricks on us,' Chloe said, trying to sound cheerful. 'Now, Morris. Do you recognise anything?'

'No,' Morris replied sadly.

THE CRYSTAL CAVE

Chloe flew even deeper into the tangle of trees.

It was very dark.

And very quiet.

Up ahead, she saw two pin-points of light coming from the trunk of a tree.

Then they disappeared.

Then they beamed brightly at her once more.

On and off, on and off the lights blinked.

Chloe's tummy gave a fearful lurch as she realised what she was looking at.

They weren't lights. They were eyes. Blinking at her out of the dark.

CHAPTER SIX
A Magical Wish

Chloe gave a meow of surprise
and fluttered on to the solid branch
of an oak tree with a tiny thud.

'Ouch,' Morris squeaked.

'Sssh,' Chloe whispered,

hardly daring to breathe.

Up above her, the eyes blinked again. Chloe gulped. Had she found the lions at last? The leaves on the tree above her started to rustle and from the darkness came a soft fluttering noise. It sounded a bit like a lion, stretching its paws and shaking out its mane. Chloe shrank back in fear as the leaves slowly parted to reveal the eyes again, growing bigger and bigger.

But, to Chloe's relief, there was no lion's mane to be seen. Instead, the eyes were framed by the feathery face of an owl.

A scarlet beak chirped a welcome.

'T'wit, t'woo! Who are YOU?'

Chloe gave a little sigh of delight. 'Magic and milkshakes,' she whispered softly to herself. 'Are you . . . are you . . . the Wise Wishing Owl?'

The owl nodded her head three times.

Morris squeaked and Chloe trembled with excitement. Never in her wildest dreams had she imagined she would come nose to beak with the most magical animal in all of Misty Wood. The Wise Wishing Owl, with her scarlet beak and feathers of gold, was the cleverest and oldest creature in the wood – as old as the most ancient

oak trees. She had the power to
make wishes come true . . . if you
were able to find her.

'You are very far from home,
little Cobweb Kitten. Are you lost?'
The Wise Wishing Owl's voice was

like the most beautiful piece of
music Chloe had ever heard.

'Yes,' Chloe said. 'I'm trying
to help this little Moss Mouse,
Morris, find his family. I've been
searching and searching but I
can't find them anywhere!' A
silvery tear ran down Chloe's
cheek and she sniffed sadly.

'There, there, little kitten,
don't cry,' the Wise Wishing Owl
said. 'You found *me*, and not many

do. Now, do you have any idea where Morris might live?'

'Yes, he says he lives by the lions,' Chloe answered with a gulp.

'The lions! The lions!' Morris squeaked.

'Oh.' The Wise Wishing Owl furrowed her feathery brow. 'I've lived in Misty Wood for a very, very long time but I'm afraid I have never heard of any lions living here.'

Chloe gave a long, sad sigh. 'That's what everyone says.'

The Wise Wishing Owl turned her head slowly from side to side three times. 'It helps me to think,' she explained when she saw Chloe staring at her. 'And now I have thought, I believe I know where Morris lives.'

'Hurray!' Morris squeaked.

'You do?' Chloe's face lit up with excitement. 'Is it very far?'

'It certainly is,' the Wise
Wishing Owl said with a nod.
'Perhaps I could have a word with
young Morris?'

Chloe tilted her head.

'Hello, Morris,' said the Wise
Wishing Owl.

'Hello,' Morris squeaked.
'I've lost my mummy and daddy.'

'I know,' said the Wise Wishing
Owl. 'Now, tell me something.
What is your dearest wish?'

'To find my mummy and daddy,' Morris said with a little sigh.

'Then I shall grant your wish,' the Wise Wishing Owl said solemnly.

'Hurray!' Morris cheered.

'Really?' Chloe asked.

'Of course,' the Wise Wishing Owl replied. 'I always help a fairy animal in need. You have done your best, Chloe, and I can see

you are very brave. But you also
look very tired. Why not leave the
rest to me?'

'Oh, yes please,' Chloe said.

'Then hold on to your whiskers!' the Wise Wishing Owl hooted. 'I'm sending you home.'

The owl flapped her huge wings up and down three times. A gentle breeze began to play around the tree branch.

Chloe felt a twig brush her face and the breeze grow stronger. She and Morris were lifted skywards. Up and up they spiralled, travelling faster with

each twist and turn. Misty Wood spun beneath them, a blur of colours and light. Chloe laughed excitedly – it was even better than sliding down the rainbow!

All of a sudden the spinning stopped and they landed with a bump on the ground, a cloud of yellow cushioning their fall.

'Lions!' Chloe gasped, her head still dizzy. But as her eyes adjusted to the bright daylight she

A MAGICAL WISH

saw they hadn't landed on the back of a fierce yellow lion, but in a field of golden dandelions.

'Lions! Lions!' Morris cried in delight.

'Sunshine and sparkles!' Chloe said with a smile. 'Look! We're in Dandelion Dell!' She stretched out on the blanket of bobbing yellow flowers. 'So, you live by the *dande*lions, Morris.'

'Yes! Yes!' Morris scampered

116

down from her back and did a cartwheel in delight.

Chloe chuckled. 'I should have known there wouldn't be any actual lions in Misty Wood.'

Just then there was a rustling sound in the dell. The dandelions started to sway. Something, or someone, was making its way towards them. Chloe heard a small, high-pitched noise, growing louder as it got nearer.

117

'Morris, Morris, Morris, MORRIS!'

Across the yellow field a procession of Moss Mice appeared, marching through the dandelions.

'Mummy, Daddy!' Morris cried, and scampered into the arms of two very relieved-looking Moss Mice. The rest of the procession cheered and waved.

Morris turned to Chloe. 'My mummy and daddy! We found them!'

A MAGICAL WISH

CHAPTER SEVEN

Home at Last!

As the Moss Mice gathered round,
Chloe told them all about her and
Morris's adventures.

'You thought we lived by
some scary lions?' Morris's

mummy said, her eyes wide.

Chloe nodded.

'And yet you still tried to find us?' Morris's daddy asked.

Chloe nodded again.

'Well then, you are a very brave Cobweb Kitten,' he said, and all of the other Moss Mice started clapping and cheering in agreement.

Morris wriggled out of his mummy's arms and scampered

back up on to Chloe's back.
'Thank you for helping me,
Chloe,' he whispered in her ear.
'I'll never forget you.'

Chloe fizzed with happiness to
the very tips of her whiskers.

Morris's daddy clapped his
paws together as Morris hopped
back down. 'Tell us, Chloe,
is there any way we can repay
you? We Moss Mice may be small
but we are very hard workers. If

there is anything you need just let us know.'

'Anything at all,' Morris's mummy added.

Chloe scratched her head.

'Thank you, but I can't think of anything I need now that Morris is safe. I suppose I'd better get back to –' Chloe gasped. 'Decorations and Dandelions! My cobwebs!'

She looked at the sun, now high in the sky. It seemed very long ago that she had woken with the sunrise and set off to get her dewdrops. 'Yes, yes, there is something you can help me with,' she said eagerly.

Chloe had never flown with so many other fairy animals before. The Moss Mice spun and tumbled through the sky like dandelion seeds scattering on the breeze.

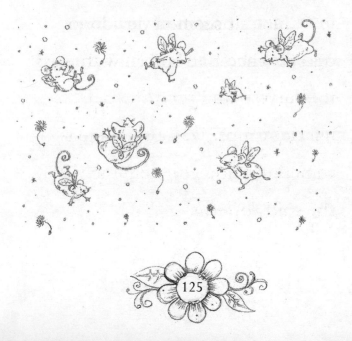

'Here we are!' Chloe cried
at last, spotting the Hawthorn
Hedgerows far below them.

In a swirl of excitement, the
Moss Mice floated down to land in
the clearing.

Chloe's basket of dewdrops
was still where she had left it, tucked

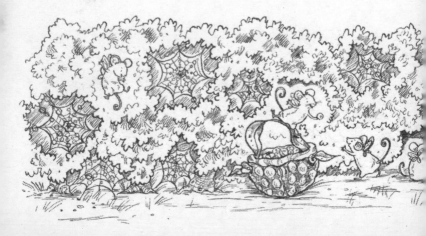

under one of the hedges. After she
had shown them what to do, the
Moss Mice set to work, singing
happy songs as they scampered
about. Soon all the cobwebs were
decorated with sparkling dewdrops
and Hawthorn Hedgerows had
never looked so beautiful.

Chloe clapped her paws with glee. 'Thank you!' she cried.

'Don't mention it,' said Morris's daddy. 'Now, after so much excitement I think we all deserve a treat.'

'Treat! Treat!' Morris cried.

'We shall have a picnic,' Morris's daddy declared and all the other mice started to cheer. 'And, Chloe, you must be our very special guest.'

Chloe was so happy she thought she might burst. What a magical day it had been. She may not have found any lions but she had certainly found plenty of new friends. It was lovely living in Misty Wood.

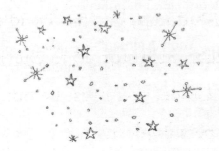

Misty Wood is home to
all sorts of **Fairy Animals**.
Which fairy animal would
you be if you lived there?
Take this fun quiz to find out!

 Misty Wood is full of beautiful things.
Which of these do you think is the prettiest?

a)   Sparkly dewdrops
b)   Velvety green moss
c)   A brightly coloured flower
d)   A floaty cloud of pollen

 Each of the **Fairy Animals** is cute and special in its
own way. If you were a fairy animal, which of these
would you most like to have?

a)   Silky fur
b)   Silver whiskers
c)   Soft, floppy ears
d)   A fluffy, waggy tail

3 Of all the lovely places in Misty Wood, which is your favourite?

a) Dewdrop Spring
b) Dandelion Dell
c) Bluebell Glade
d) Honeydew Meadow

4 The **Fairy Animals** stay cosy and warm at night. If you were a fairy animal, where would you like to sleep?

a) In a cosy cot of moss and soft grass
b) In a snuggly bed under an oak tree
c) In a lovely warm warren beneath a cluster of mulberry bushes
d) In a sweet little den under a hawthorn hedge

5 The **Fairy Animals** all have a favourite thing to do in Misty Wood. What do you like doing the most?

a) Decorating things and making everything around you look pretty
b) Using your imagination to make things
c) Playing with beautiful flowers
d) Running, jumping, telling jokes and playing games

Mostly a

You would be a Cobweb Kitten! Cobweb Kittens love pretty things, especially the glittery dewdrops they decorate the Misty Wood cobwebs with. They enjoy collecting things in their baskets and love drinking milk.

Mostly b

You would be a Moss Mouse! Moss Mice can be quite shy and quiet. They love stories and having cuddles on the soft green cushions they make.

Mostly c

You would be a Bud Bunny! Bud Bunnies have cute floppy ears and soft pink noses. They love playing outside in the sunshine with their friends, especially amongst flowers.

Mostly d

You would be a Pollen Puppy! Pollen Puppies have loads of energy and like to run about. They also love having fun and making the other fairy animals laugh.

Misty Wood Treasure Hunt

Misty Wood is full of treasures, from the moonbeams in Moonshine Pond, to a cave made of crystal and a rainbow you can slide down. Can you find the following treasures in your park or garden?

 A lovely green leaf

A bright yellow dandelion

A pretty feather

A piece of velvety moss

A prickly pine cone

A snowy white daisy

Wise Owl Wishes

'T'wit, t'woo! I am the Wise Wishing Owl. I live in the Heart of Misty Wood. Not many people find me, but those who do may ask me to grant them their wishes.'

If you could have three wishes granted by the Wise Wishing Owl, what would they be? You can write them down here:

A wish for my best friend:

_____

A wish for my mum:

_____

A wish just for me:

_____

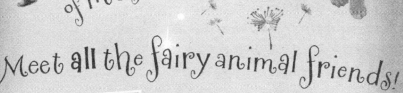

Fairy Animals
of Misty Wood

Meet **all** the fairy animal friends!

Look out for Hailey the Hedgehog
and lots more coming soon...

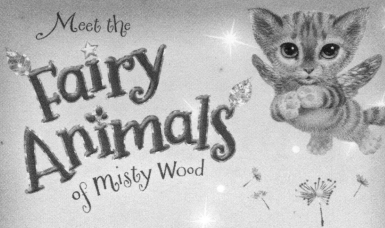

Meet the

Fairy Animals

of Misty Wood

There's a whole world to explore!

Download the FREE *Fairy Animals* app and visit **fairyanimals.com** for lots of gorgeous goodies . . .

- Free stuff
- Games
- Write to your favourite characters
- Step inside Misty Wood
- Send us your cute pet pictures
- Make your own fairy wings!